Written by Dr. Barbara Howard
Illustrated by Siddhant Jumde

ISBN: 978-1-957922-30-0
Edition: July 2022

For all inquiries, please contact us at:
info@puppysmiles.org

To see more of our books, visit us at:
www.PuppyDogsAndIceCream.com

This book is given with love

To _____

From _____

Introduction to "Will Won't Go to School"

This is a story about a boy named William who discovers that being at school on his own is not scary, but fun! Lots of young children worry about being away from their parents and facing new things when they start school. William's mother wisely supports her son by going with him to school and easing him in at first, and by telling him about all the positive experiences that come with a school environment. The natural attractions of other kids and fun activities quickly take over William's fears as he makes this important transition.

As a Developmental-Behavioral Pediatrician expert in the emotional development of children, I love how this book reassures children that they can adjust. Perhaps, more importantly, it also models for parents how acceptance of a child's fears and initial unambivalent support facilitate development of the ability to separate and grow while strengthening trust in the parent-child relationship.

As Assistant Professor of Pediatrics at Johns Hopkins and in practice, I have studied and coached many families through anxiety issues of both children and parents with strategies that promote emotional health long term. Working through the dysfunction anxiety can produce is readily done, but is done more easily if the signs of anxiety are detected and addressed early. This is especially important in order to avoid actions well-meaning parents may take such as shaming or forcing children through their fears.

But child anxiety can sometimes be invisible to adults and to physicians... For this reason I, along with my pediatrician husband, created the CHADIS web-based system to allow screening questionnaires for anxiety and many other physical and mental health conditions to be done online before regular checkups. It includes evidence-based guidance for clinicians to support families and refers families to specialists. With the tools of both CHADIS and this book, I hope you and your children enjoy and are able to work through the first day jitters!

- Dr. Barbara Howard

Will's first day of school was approaching **too fast**.
He would join other children, no parents at last.
Inside, Will felt **nervous, anxious, and afraid**,
To be in a new place, and start a new grade.

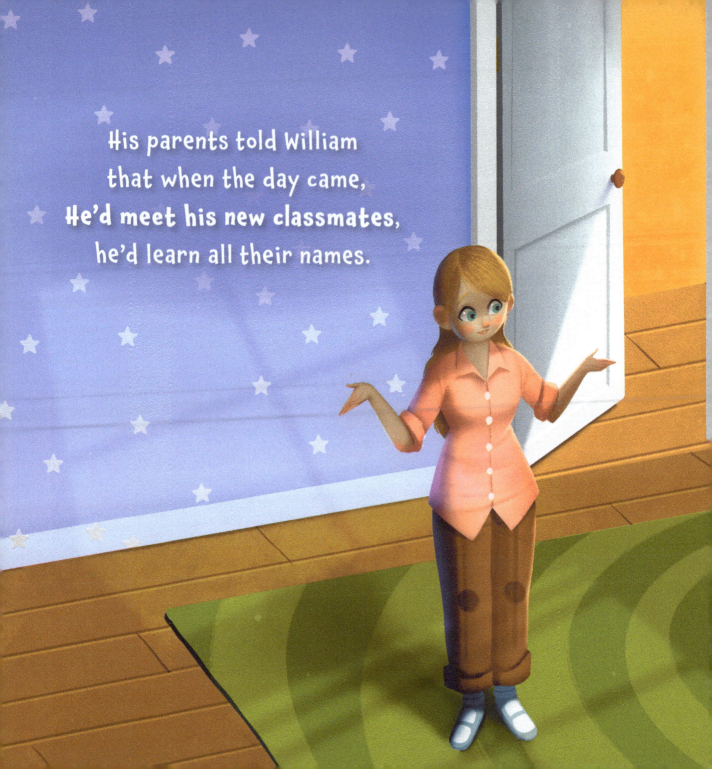

His parents told William
that when the day came,
He'd meet his new classmates,
he'd learn all their names.

But William did not
feel much better at all,
His belly felt knotted,
his voice came out small.

At home, **he felt comfy** – he had all his toys.
How would he make friends with new girls and boys?

What would the days hold? **He'd miss Mom and Dad.**
What could be better than days they'd all had?

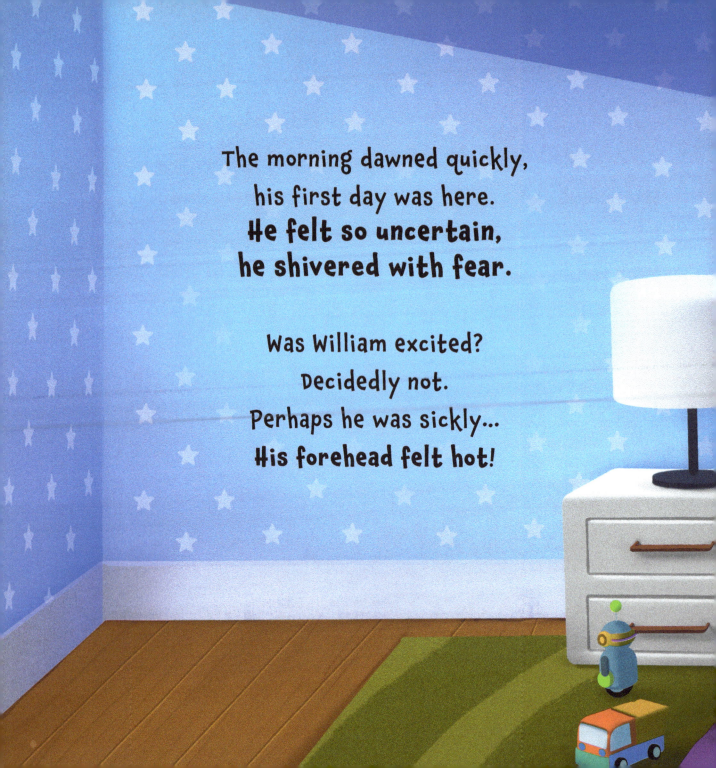

The morning dawned quickly,
his first day was here.
**He felt so uncertain,
he shivered with fear.**

Was William excited?
Decidedly not.
Perhaps he was sickly...
His forehead felt hot!

Will pulled up the covers,
right over his head,
And squeaked out, **"Hey Mommy,
let's stay home instead."**

Mom sat on the edge
of his bed and said, "Will,
I know that you're frightened,
but this is a skill..."

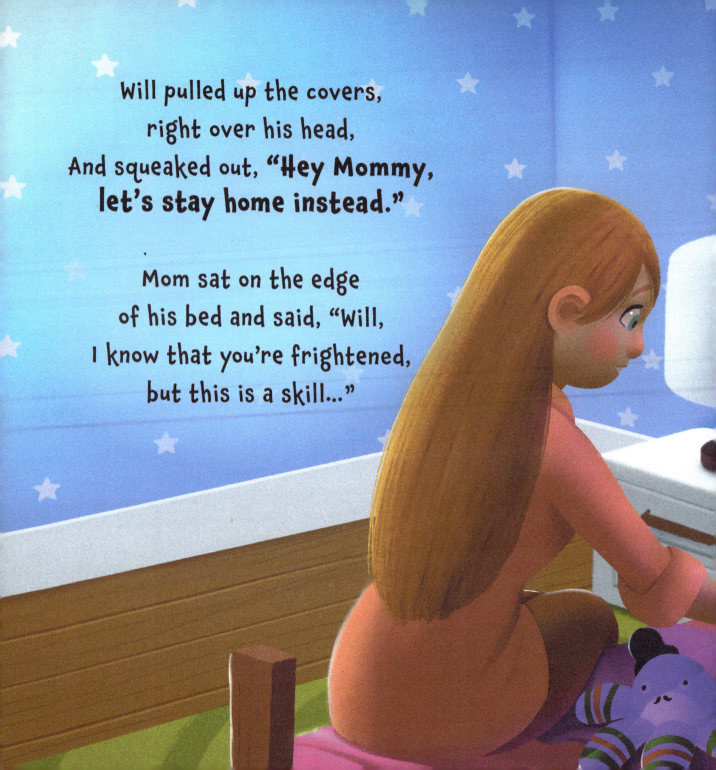

"Staying home with your parents
is easy, it's true,
But we can do hard things,
I know you can, too.

Your home is familiar,
but life holds much more.
This chapter's exciting,
you'll never be bored!"

"At home with your parents, your circle is small.
There's just us to play with, inside of these walls.
At school, you'll be challenged, each day will be new.
There are many adventures that wait there for you.

Then Mom said "Get going,
we shouldn't be late,
You'll see when we get there...
it's going to be great!"

William and Mommy walked
through the big door,
There were so many faces,
Will still felt unsure...

"This is your teacher,
your friend every day.
She'll teach you new skill sets,
and new ways to play."

The classroom had posters
and art on the walls,
Mom gave Will a squeeze,
then walked out to the hall.

Will suddenly panicked, he wanted to cry.
He had never been happy with saying "goodbye!"

His teacher said, "William, we're happy you're here."
And her smile **helped a little** to lessen his fear.

"Please sit next to Jessie, it's her first day, too."
And Will realized Jessie might also feel blue.

The teacher said
"We'll make FunDoh,
in red, blue and green...

We'll mix crazy colors that you've never seen!"

Then, Will and his classmate both made a bright ball,
And Will thought of Mommy... barely at all!

Next, there came reading,
with stories to tell.
His teacher did voices,
she acted so well!

2+2=?

Then science, and math time,
with volcanoes to make...
They played in the kitchen,
and they served magic cake!

At lunchtime Will thought,
in a moment of calm,
"I've been far too busy
to miss Dad or Mom.

I was scared for this first day,
and it's not even done,
But so far it seems like
this school thing is fun!"

"At home I get lonely,
sure Mom's there, too,
But here in the classroom,
there's so much to do!"

Then, there came recess,
where they all ran outside,
Will made some new friends
and slid down the slide.

They played cops and robbers,
then rockets in space.
**Will realized he really
could like this new place.**

They traded at snack time,
Will tried a friend's treat.
"At home," pondered William,
"We don't have this to eat."

The day was soon over,
it really flew by.
Will rushed to his mother,
and said "I didn't cry!"

The next morning, he woke up excited for school.
He hoped that the lessons would be just as cool.

At breakfast, Mom asked,
"What was your favorite part?"
Will thought very hard, then said, "I loved art!"

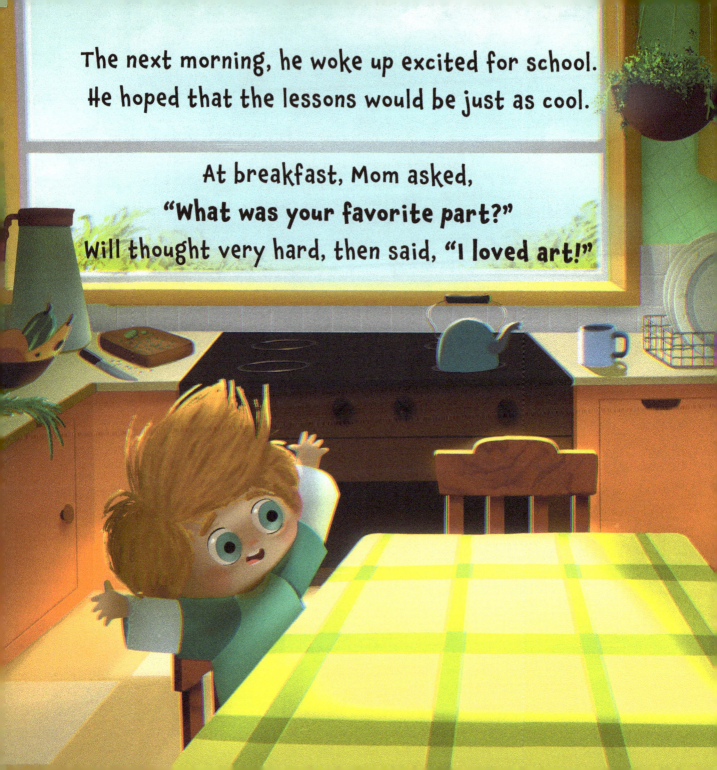

Soon, Will didn't worry
about each new day.
He realized that changes
could turn out okay.

Home had his parents,
he loved Mom and Dad,
But school was just "different",
and different's not bad!

KINDERGARTEN

Life's an adventure right out of a book —
It's full of new wonders, if only you'll look.
Each stage has its chapter, and each chapter must end,
You continue to read to see what's 'round the bend.

If something's not safe parents say how to beware,
So you can adventure without any care!
Change can feel scary, and challenges great,
But school's a new chapter that life can create.

Will's parents would be there
if he felt lonely or sad,
But adventure is out there
and ready to be had!

Claim your FREE Gift!

 Visit:

PDICBooks.com/Gift

Thank you for purchasing

Will Won't
GO TO SCHOOL

and welcome to the Puppy Dogs & Ice Cream family.
We're certain you're going to love the little gift
we've prepared for you at the website above.

CPSIA information can be obtained
at www.ICGtesting.com
Printed in the USA
BVHW012308270223
659257BV00006B/40

9 781957 922300